The ArtScroll Children's Holiday Series

6

Yaffa Ganz

PESACH

WITH BINA, BENNY AND CHAGGAI HAYONAH

Illustrated by Liat Benyaminy Ariel

© Copyright 1991, 2006, 2013 by MESORAH PUBLICATIONS, Ltd. and YAFFA GANZ
4401 Second Avenue / Brooklyn, N.Y. 11232 / (718) 921-9000
Printed in the United States of America by Noble Book Press Corp.

Shalom! It's springtime and I'm Chaggai HaYonah — Chaggai the holiday dove. Tomorrow night is the 15th of Nissan, the night of the first Seder and the beginning of the holiday of Pesach. My friends Bina and Benny and I have been helping Imma clean the house. It's a big job, too!"

"But we're finished now!" said Bina, waving a rag. "Everything is bright and shiny and ready for the Seder!"

"It sure is," said Benny. "There's not a drop of *chametz* left in the entire house. Even Chaggai will have to eat matzah crumbs from now on."

"Matzah crumbs? That won't bother me one bit. It's a pleasure to eat matzah crumbs when Pesach comes. And now that we've

cleaned out the closets, arranged all the drawers,
polished the candlesticks,
scrubbed all the floors,
vacuumed the carpets, our pockets, and books,
checked under and over in crannies and nooks;

"We can finally …"
"Rest!" said Benny, dropping into a chair.
"Oh no! Not yet!" cried Bina.

"Why not? The kitchen is spotless from top to bottom. The Pesach dishes and pots and pans are on the shelves. And Imma is already cooking gefilte fish! What else is there to do before we're ready for the Seder?"

"One thing," said Chaggai, "is to make sure we know the difference between *chametz* and matzah."

"That's easy!" answered Benny.

He stood up and cleared his throat. Then he began, "CHAMETZ — There are five different kinds of grain that can become *chametz*.

chitah	wheat
kusemes	spelt
seorah	barley
shifon	rye
shiboles-shual	oats

"If water is mixed with flour made from any of these five grains and is left to stand for more than 18 minutes, the dough becomes *chametz*. During the entire holiday of Pesach (which is seven days in the Land of Israel and eight days in other places) we aren't allowed to own any *chametz* or eat any food which has *chametz* in it. That's why we don't eat bread on Pesach."

"And matzah," continued Bina, "is just the opposite. Matzah is baked so quickly that it takes less than 18 minutes from the time water is added to the flour until the dough is rolled out, punched full of holes, popped into the oven, baked, and taken out, all ready to eat. Matzah is called *lechem oni* — poor man's bread — because it's only flour and water, baked very very quickly, and not allowed to rise and puff up like regular bread." Bina stopped to catch her breath.

"Matzah is one of the most important mitzvos of Pesach!" said Benny. "We don't eat any on erev Pesach, so that the taste of the matzah will be new and delicious on the night of the Seder! But I still want to know what else we have to do tonight and tomorrow."

"Tsk, tsk tsk," chirped Chaggai. "You must be very tired if you've forgotten what has to be done on erev Pesach! Let's see now … your father has already taken care of …
MECHIRAS CHAMETZ — Selling the *Chametz*. You don't want to own any *chametz* during Pesach! And tonight, erev Pesach, you will help him with …
BEDIKAS CHAMETZ — The Search for the *Chametz*.

"You'll search carefully all through the house to make sure every last drop of *chametz* is gone. Then, tomorrow morning you will go outside with your father for …
BIYUR CHAMETZ — Burning the *Chametz*.

"And then you will have a completely *chametz*-free, spotlessly clean, kosher-for-Pesach house!"

"Well then," said Bina, "we'd better hurry and put out ten pieces of bread or cookies for *bedikas chametz*, or Abba may not find any!"

Early the next morning, Bina and Benny watched as their father burned the *chametz* in the backyard. As soon as he finished, they went into the kitchen and began preparing the *ke'arah* — the Seder plate. Here's what they put on it:

ZE'ROAH (a roasted bone) to remind us of the *Korban Pesach* — the Pesach offering that was roasted and eaten on Pesach night

BEITZAH (a roasted egg) to remind us of the *Korban Chagigah*, the special holiday offering brought with the *Korban Pesach* in the *Beis Hamikdash*

MAROR (bitter herbs) to remind us how bitter it was to be a slave in Egypt

CHAROSES (a mixture of apples, nuts, spices and wine) to remind us of the bricks the Jews were forced to make in Egypt

KARPAS (parsley or some other vegetable which will be dipped into salt water) to make the children at the table curious so they will ask more questions about the Seder

CHAZERES (a second bitter herb)

THE KE'ARAH — The Seder Plate

e've done it!" said Bina with a smile. "Even Chaggai will agree — we're finally ready for the Seder!"

"It's about time too! After all the work we've done, I almost feel like a slave myself! I wonder what the Jews in Egypt felt like on erev Pesach," said Benny.

"I can tell you that!" said Chaggai. "My father told me, and his father told him before that. Fathers have been telling the story to their children for more than 3300 years."

There had been a terrible famine in the Land of Israel. Yaakov Avinu had taken his family — seventy people in all — and gone down to Egypt where his son Yosef was second in command to Pharaoh himself. Pharaoh welcomed the Jews and gave them the Land of Goshen to live in. As long as Yosef was alive, the Jews fared well.

But when Yosef died and Pharaoh saw that the Jews had become a mighty nation, he was afraid they might

someday rebel against the Egyptians. He decided to turn the Jews into slaves. He made them pay high taxes and forced them to do hard, heavy work. He made them build cities and work in the fields for the Egyptians.

Finally, when Pharaoh saw that even the hard work did not keep the Jews from growing and multiplying, he commanded the Jewish midwives to kill all Jewish baby boys as soon as they were born! But the midwives weren't afraid of Pharaoh and they didn't listen. So Pharaoh decreed that the babies be taken away from their mothers and thrown into the Nile River.

"Oh," Bina shuddered. "How awful! Poor babies! Poor mothers!"

Pharaoh thought that he could do anything he wanted to do. But there was one woman who didn't agree. Her name was Yocheved, daughter of Levi, granddaughter of Yaakov Avinu. Yocheved was one of the midwives who had saved other people's babies, and she surely wasn't going to give her own child to the Egyptians! When her son Moshe was born, Yocheved hid him for three months. Then she put him in a small reed basket and placed the basket in the river, trusting that Hashem would save him.

"I know what happened then," said Benny. "Pharaoh's daughter came down to the river and found Moshe. She brought him into the royal palace and raised him as her own son."

"And do you know who helped her?" asked Chaggai. "Yocheved, Moshe's mother! Moshe's sister Miriam had waited near the river to see what would happen. When Pharaoh's daughter found the basket, Miriam said she knew of a wonderful nursemaid for the baby. And she did! She brought her own mother."

"Miriam was smart," said Benny. "She knew that if Yocheved took care of Moshe, he would never forget that he was a Jew."

One day, when Moshe was a young man, he saw an Egyptian taskmaster beating a helpless Jewish slave. Moshe killed the cruel Egyptian. Pharaoh was furious. Even Pharaoh's daughter wasn't able to help Moshe, so he ran away to the land of Midian to save his life.

For many years, Moshe was a shepherd in Midian. One day, as he was searching for a lost lamb, he saw a bush on fire, but it wasn't burning up! Moshe came closer to look at it, when suddenly, he heard the voice of G-d calling to him from the bush.

"Moshe! Moshe!" called G-d.

"Hineni!" answered a trembling Moshe. "I am here and ready to do Your bidding, Hashem."

G-d told Moshe that the time had come to take the Jews out of Egypt and bring them back to the Land of Israel. And Moshe was the one He had chosen to do the job!

"I wish I had a chance to do a job like that!" said Benny.

"Maybe you think so now, but I bet you wouldn't think so if you had to go to the royal palace and stand up to Pharaoh!" said Bina. "Pharaoh didn't like Moshe one bit!"

"No, he didn't," agreed Chaggai. "But Moshe and his brother Aharon went anyway."

They told Pharaoh, "G-d has commanded the Jews to leave Egypt for three days and worship Him in the desert. Let us go!"

Pharaoh was so angry that he decided to make the Jews work even harder. From then on, not only would they have to make bricks to build with; they would even have to collect the straw in order to make the bricks!

Moshe warned Pharaoh that G-d would punish him if he didn't allow the Jews to leave, but Pharaoh just laughed. He was sure that his magicians were stronger than Hashem. And so all through the land of Egypt, in every place except Goshen, where the Jews lived, the Ten Plagues began.

1. Blood — דָּם

First, all the water in the land of Egypt turned into blood. The Egyptians couldn't drink or cook or wash. The only way they could have water was by buying it from a Jew.

2. Frogs — צְפַרְדֵּעַ

Next, came the frogs. They were all over the country. In beds and dishes, on tables and chairs and floors, slimy frogs were everywhere. The sound of their croaking drove the Egyptians crazy!

3. Lice — כִּנִּים

Then lice came crawling up from the ground and into people's clothing and hair. The Egyptians were sick and sore from itching and scratching, but Pharaoh was stubborn. He would not let the Jews go!

4. Wild Animals — עָרוֹב

Hordes of savage animals suddenly appeared. They ran wild, killing and destroying everything in their path. Again, only the Jews in Goshen were spared.

5. Pestilence — דֶבֶּר

The Egyptians' animals — their cattle and sheep and their beautiful horses, the pride and joy of Egypt — sickened and died.

6. Boils — שְׁחִין

Now everyone in Egypt was covered with horrible, painful blisters and boils! They couldn't stand, couldn't sit, couldn't lie down. The suffering was terrible. And still, Pharaoh refused to let the Jews go.

7. Hail — בָּרָד

Then, a horrendous hail storm swept across Egypt. Enormous pieces of ice with flashes of fire inside destroyed all the flowers, the gardens, and the trees.

8. Locusts — אַרְבֶּה

And the locusts came — millions and millions of them, in great, dark, buzzing clouds. They swept across Egypt like a razor, mowing down and gobbling up the grain and crops in the fields.

9. Darkness — חֹשֶׁךְ

An inky black darkness, so thick that no candle or fire or lamp could shine through, covered the country. The Egyptians sat glued to their chairs or lay trembling in their beds.

10. Firstborn — מַכַּת בְּכוֹרוֹת

Finally, at midnight, on the 15th of Nissan, death struck the land of Egypt. Every first-born man, boy, and beast died. Egypt was filled with cries and weeping.

But in Goshen, the Jews rejoiced. In Goshen, the Angel of Death passed over every Jewish house. Not a single person died.

In the middle of the night, Pharaoh called Moshe, "Quickly!" he cried. "Leave Egypt — you and your people and your cattle and your sheep! Hurry! Before we all die!"

The mighty Pharaoh was defeated at last.

"How did the Angel of Death know which houses belonged to the Jews?" asked Bina.

Chaggai stretched his wings and shook his feathers before answering, "He had a clear sign."

On erev Pesach, the 14th of Nissan, each Jewish family slaughtered and roasted a lamb for the Pesach sacrifice. They smeared the blood of the lamb on the *mashkof* and the *mezuzos* — the tops and the sides of the doorways of their homes. When Hashem came down to slay all firstborn Egyptians, He passed over every house where the doorway was smeared with blood.

The Jews celebrated their first Pesach. They roasted their lambs and ate the meat with matzah and bitter herbs. They ate in great haste, fully dressed and ready to leave, for soon — any minute now — it would be time to go.

All night long, the Jews waited and rejoiced. Early in the morning, and the moment finally came. Carrying their children, their belongings, their walking sticks, the matzos they had prepared, and the gold and silver gifts the Egyptians had given them, they began to move. With a mighty hand and an outstretched arm, with miracles and wondrous deeds, G-d was taking them out of Egypt.

The long march began. The Jews had no food except their hastily baked matzos. Yet they followed Moshe faithfully into the desert. Nor did they forget their ancestor Yosef. Just as they had promised long ago, they carried his coffin out of Egypt, all the way to Eretz Yisrael.

"How did they know which way to go?" asked Benny.

They followed a heavenly sign that showed them. A pillar of cloud moved before them, leading them by day. At night a pillar of fire came to give them light. For forty years, hundreds of thousands of Jews walked under G-d's Clouds of Glory through the desert. It was a wonderful sight.

But soon after the Jews were gone, Pharaoh changed his mind again, and before you knew it, he was chasing them with his soldiers and chariots.

The chariots didn't do the Egyptians any good. When the Jews reached the shores of the Yam Suf — the Reed Sea — they began to complain. The Egyptians were coming up behind them; the water was in front! What were they to do? Did they leave Egypt only to be killed in the desert?

Then G-d spoke to Moshe. "Lift up your staff," Hashem commanded. "Stretch your hand out over the sea and split it open! The Children of Israel shall pass through the midst of the sea on dry land!"

The Jews all stood there and waited, but nothing happened. How could they enter the water if it didn't split? The people were frightened. But one man, Nachshon ben Aminadav, jumped into the water and went forward while everyone else waited on the shore and watched. Just when they were sure that Nachshon would drown, the waters split open! They piled up into mighty, watery walls, leaving a safe, dry passage in the middle.

Suddenly, the pillar of cloud moved back until it was standing between the Jews and the Egyptians. There it remained, like a fiery guard, until all the Jews had safely crossed the sea.

When the Egyptians reached the shores of the sea and saw the water split wide open, they plunged in with their horses and chariots. But they didn't make it! The waters came crashing down and every single one, except for Pharaoh himself, was killed!

Then Moshe and the Jewish people sang *Az Yashir*, a Song of Thanksgiving to Hashem! And Miriam took her tambourine and sang and danced with the women!

"I wish I could have been there," sighed Bina.

"So do I," said Benny.

"You know, it's too bad the Jews didn't have wings, like a dove," suggested Chaggai. "Then they could have flown right out of Egypt and across the water to safety."

"They had something better than wings," said Bina. "They had Hashem!"

"Wouldn't it be wonderful if we could offer the *Korban Pesach* in the *Beis Hamikdash* today?" asked Bina.

"Maybe, but we can't," answered a practical Benny, "so let's concentrate on the main mitzvos of the Seder!"

> DRINKING FOUR CUPS OF WINE — to remember the four ways G-d promised to redeem us.
>
> MAGGID — reading the *Haggadah* and telling the story of Pesach.
>
> EATING MATZAH — while leaning to one side, just like kings eating in a very relaxed, unhurried way.
>
> EATING MAROR — bitter herbs — to remind us that we weren't always like kings. We started out as slaves until Hashem took us out of Egypt!

"My favorite part of the *Haggadah* is the Four Sons! The Wise Son, the Evil Son, the Simple Son and the Son Who Couldn't Even Ask a Question!" said Benny.

"And the songs," said Bina. "Don't forget all the wonderful songs we sing! *Chad Gadya*, the One Kid who is really the Jewish people. And *Echad Mi Yodea*, Who Knows One. And *Dayeinu!*"

"I wonder why there is no Chad Yonah, one dove, in the *Haggadah*," said Chaggai. "The Jewish people are often compared to a dove."

"Well," answered Benny, "after the Seder we read *Shir HaShirim*, and doves are mentioned there lots of times!"

Bina nodded her head in agreement and Chaggai looked pleased.

"In that case," he said, "I think we're just about ready for the Seder."

"Let's check again," said Bina, "just to make sure. Is the wine on the table? And the three matzos? And is everything on the *ke'arah*?"

"The table is perfect," said Benny. "It's time to get dressed. Then Imma will light the candles and we'll go to shul with Abba. And when we come back, Abba will put on his white *kittel* and we can begin!

"I just wish ..." mumbled Benny.

"You just wish what?" asked Bina and Chaggai together.

"I just wish I could ask the *Mah Nishtanah* for a change. Bina always gets to ask the Four Questions because she's the youngest!"

"But you always find the *Afikoman*!" said Bina.

"Why don't you take turns?" asked Chaggai. "On the first night of Pesach, at the first Seder, Bina can ask the *Mah Nishtanah* and Benny can look for the *Afikoman*. At the second Seder, you can switch!"

"And we can both open the door for Eliyahu *Hanavi* both nights!" said Bina. "You're such a smart dove, Chaggai!"

"Why, thank you!" said the dove. "And just to help you remember everything in the proper order, here's a list of the things we do at the Seder."

THE ORDER OF THE SEDER

KADESH: Recite *Kiddush* on the wine

UR'CHATZ: Wash your hands without saying a *berachah*

KARPAS: Dip a vegetable into salt water, make a *berachah* and eat it

YACHATZ: Break the middle matzah and hide the bigger piece for the *Afikoman*

MAGGID: Tell the story of Pesach and read the *Haggadah*

RACHTZAH: Wash you hands and say a *berachah*, before eating the matzah

MOTZI: Make the *Hamotzi* blessing

MATZAH: Make the blessing on the matzah and eat it

MAROR: Make the blessing on the *maror* and eat it

KORECH: Eat a "sandwich" of matzah and bitter herbs

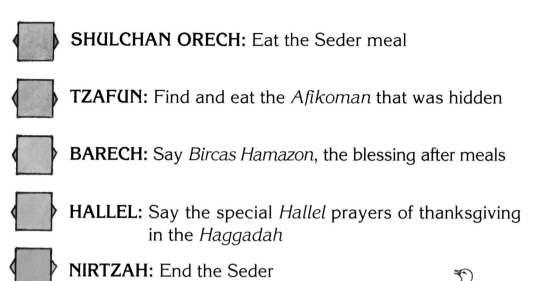

SHULCHAN ORECH: Eat the Seder meal

TZAFUN: Find and eat the *Afikoman* that was hidden

BARECH: Say *Bircas Hamazon*, the blessing after meals

HALLEL: Say the special *Hallel* prayers of thanksgiving in the *Haggadah*

NIRTZAH: End the Seder

"One last thing," said Chaggai. "On the second day of Pesach, the Jews brought the *Omer*, an offering of the new barley they had just harvested, to the *Beis Hamikdash*. And on the second night of Pesach, we begin *Sefiras Ha'Omer*, the Counting of the *Omer*. We count each day and week for 49 days — a full seven weeks. Do you know why?"

"We're counting the days until the holiday of Shavuos — the giving of the Torah at *Har Sinai*!" said Benny. "And Shavuos is the 50th day after Pesach!"

"I'm glad we begin counting the *Omer* on the second night of Pesach, not the first," said Bina. "We have enough things to remember tonight! Come on, Benny. Let's get dressed. It's almost time for Imma to light the candles. Pesach is about to begin!"

idn't we have a lovely Seder, Benny?" Bina yawned. It was a rather long yawn. Bina was a very sleepy sister. Even Chaggai looked a bit droopy.

"It sure was," said Benny. "And you know, Bina, you were right. It would be wonderful if we could offer the *Korban Pesach* in the *Beis Hamikdash* and eat it in Yerushalayim."

"We will, someday soon. You'll see," said Bina, yawning again.

"I know. That's why, every year at the Seder, we say —

This year we are here,
but next year may we be in the Land of Israel.

Someday, we will be back in Jerusalem, all the Jewish people ..."

But Bina didn't answer. She was fast asleep, dreaming about kids and lambs and doves and simple sons and seas that split open and giant matzos. Before you could say *Chad Gadya*, Benny's eyes were closed too.

Chaggai gave a small dove-like yawn and fluffed his feathers.

חַג כָּשֵׁר וְשָׂמֵחַ

Chag Kasher V'same'ach

A kosher and joyful holiday to you all, from Bina and Benny and from me, Chaggai the holiday dove. And of course,

לְשָׁנָה הַבָּאָה בִּירוּשָׁלַיִם

May next year be in Jerusalem!

Chaggai puffed himself up into a soft round ball, tucked his head under his wing and went straight to sleep.

GLOSSARY

Afikoman — matzah hidden until the end of the Seder
Beis Hamikdash — the Holy Temple of Jerusalem
chametz — leaven
Eliyahu Hanavi — Elijah the Prophet
erev Pesach — the day before Pesach
Haggadah — the story of Pesach read at the Seder
Har Sinai — Mount Sinai
Hashem — G-d
ke'arah — the Seder plate with the six ritual items
Korban Pesach — the Passover sacrifice in the Temple
Mah Nishtanah — the Four Questions
maror — bitter herbs
matzah — unleavened bread
mezuzah — doorpost
mitzvah, mitzvos — commandment, commandments
Pesach — Passover
Pharaoh — ruler of Egypt
Seder — the ceremony of reading the *Haggadah* and eating the holiday meal on the first two nights of Passover (in the Land Israel, on the first night)
Shir HaShirim — Song of Songs, by King Solomon
Yaakov Avinu — Our father Jacob
Yerushalayim — Jerusalem
Yosef — Joseph, the son of Jacob